Franklin's Class Trip

Dedicated with appreciation to the
Royal Ontario Museum — P.B. & B.C.

Franklin is a trademark of Kids Can Press Ltd.

Story written by Paulette Bourgeois and Sharon Jennings.
Interior illustrations prepared with the assistance of Shelley Southern.

Kids Can Press acknowledges the financial support of the Ontario Arts
Council, the Canada Council for the Arts and the Government of
Canada, through the BPIDP, for our publishing activity.

Kids Can Press Ltd.
29 Birch Avenue
Toronto, Ontario, Canada
M4V 1E2

Printed in Hong Kong by Wing King Tong Co. Ltd.

CDN PA 99 0 9 8 7 6 5

Canadian Cataloguing in Publication Data

Bourgeois, Paulette
    Franklin's class trip

ISBN 1-55074-470-4 (bound)   ISBN 1-55074-472-0 (pbk.)

I. Clark, Brenda.   II. Title.

PS8553.085477F736 1999   jC813'.54   C98-931810-9
PZ7.B68Fr 1999

Kids Can Press is a Nelvana company

Franklin's Class Trip

Written by Paulette Bourgeois
Illustrated by Brenda Clark

Kids Can Press

FRANKLIN could count by twos and tie his shoes. He had gone with his class to the bakery, the fire station and the pet store. Today Franklin's class was going to the museum. Franklin was so excited that he could hardly eat his breakfast.

The museum had lots of steps and huge doors.
"Wow, it's big," said Franklin.
"It has to be," said Beaver. "There are real
dinosaurs inside."

Beaver had been to the museum before. She knew everything about it.

"*Big* dinosaurs," she emphasized. "So big that they ate trees for breakfast."

Franklin was afraid to ask what dinosaurs ate for lunch.

Franklin sat down on the steps.

"What's wrong?" asked Snail.

"Beaver says there are real dinosaurs in the museum."

Snail looked alarmed. "That sounds scary."

Franklin nodded.

In the museum lobby, Mr. Owl went over the rules. No shouting. No running. And stay with the group.

"Mr. Owl," said Beaver, "one more thing. Watch out for dinosaurs."

Moose and Bear laughed.

Franklin didn't. He moved a little closer to Mr. Owl.

Their first stop was the bat cave.

It was dark inside. Squeaks and squawks filled the air.

"What's that?" asked Franklin.

Beaver giggled. "That's the sound bats make to find their way around."

Franklin was relieved that it was bats and not dinosaurs.

The class visited the rain forest next.
Franklin climbed high into a tree house.
He could see the tops of trees.
"Can you spot any dinosaurs?" asked Snail.
Franklin shook his head and climbed
down quickly.

There was so much to do in the museum that Franklin almost forgot about the dinosaurs.

In the medieval room, Franklin had fun dressing up like a knight.

Franklin even got to dig in a sandy pit.
He was the first one to find an arrowhead.
It was just like being a real archaeologist.

"The best part is still to come," said Beaver
as they sat down in the cafeteria.

"Yes," agreed Bear. "Lunch!"

Mr. Owl smiled. "I think Beaver means the
dinosaur exhibit."

Franklin gulped. "I'm too tired to see more.
I'll just stay here for a while," he muttered.

"Me too," said Snail.

"You'll forget about being tired when you see
the dinosaurs," said Mr. Owl. "Eat up and let's go."

Reluctantly, Franklin and Snail followed
giant footprints down a long, leafy corridor.
There was a loud roar. The floor shook.
So did Franklin.

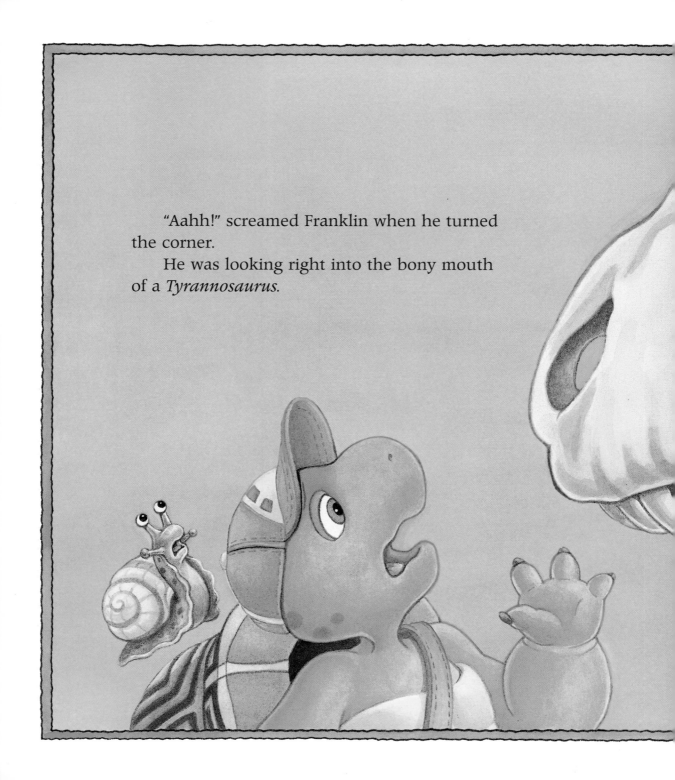

"Aahh!" screamed Franklin when he turned the corner.

He was looking right into the bony mouth of a *Tyrannosaurus*.

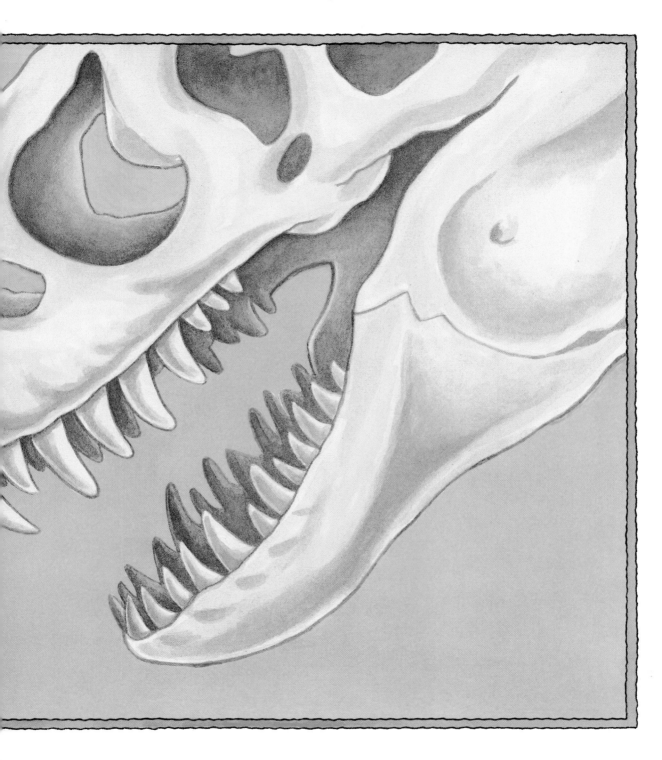

Franklin blinked. "They're bones! Real dinosaur bones! But the dinosaurs aren't alive."

"Alive?" giggled Beaver. "Of course not. There hasn't been a live dinosaur for millions of years. You make good jokes, Franklin."

"You sure do," whispered Snail.

As they were leaving, Franklin and his friends walked past the Egyptian exhibit.

"Next time," said Beaver, "you should visit the tomb. There's a mummy inside."

"Is it real?" asked Franklin.

"Yes, and scary," said Beaver.

But Franklin wasn't scared. He had a mummy at home.

And he could hardly wait to tell her all about his adventures at the museum.